Gulliver's Travels

Based on the book by

Jonathan Swift

Adapted by Gill Harvey

Illustrated by Peter Dennis

Reading consultant: Alison Kelly
Roehampton University of Surrey

Contents

Chapter 1 All so small   3

Chapter 2 The emperor   13

Chapter 3 Freedom   19

Chapter 4 War!   30

Chapter 5 Gulliver in danger   42

Chapter 6 Escape plans   53

Chapter 1

All so small

Lemuel Gulliver loved to travel and he loved adventures. This is the story of one of his stranger adventures.

It began when Gulliver boarded a ship for the Far East...

The voyage was a difficult and dangerous one. Winds howled, storms raged and the ship was pushed off course. Finally, it hit some rocks and sank.

The passengers were desperate. Some tried to escape in a small boat. But it capsized and they all drowned... except for Gulliver.

Gulliver swam for his life.
Just as he was giving up hope,
he saw land. He stumbled ashore
and collapsed on the beach.
Soon, he was fast asleep.

Where am I?
What's going on?

When he woke up, he couldn't
move – not even his head. He was
tied to the ground.

Gulliver tugged his hair free and looked around. An amazing sight met his eyes. Tiny men were clambering all over him.

"Hey!" Gulliver shouted.

What are you doing?

The men jumped off in fright. Some of them fired arrows, which pricked his skin like needles.

"Ow!" cried Gulliver. "That hurts!"

7

What were they going to do next? He soon found out. They stopped firing arrows and built a ladder beside him. Then an important-looking man climbed up and shouted in his ear.

But Gulliver didn't understand a word. He was hungry, too, so he pointed to his mouth.

"Hungry," he said.

The man must have understood him because a crowd appeared, carrying huge amounts of very small food. Gulliver gobbled it all.

Then they brought barrels of wine which Gulliver gulped down thirstily. The people gave each other sly smiles.

Unknown to Gulliver, they had put something in the wine. In seconds, he fell into a deep sleep. The people set to work.

Five hundred tiny carpenters built a wooden cart, and dragged Gulliver onto it. Then he was pulled away.

Gulliver woke up outside a magnificent temple. He was in the country's capital city, Milando. The people thought the temple could be his new home.

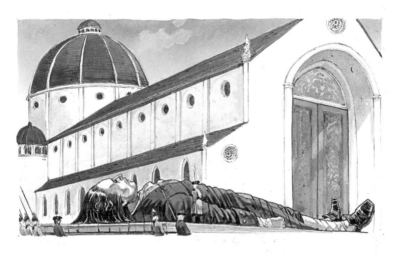

But Gulliver, who still couldn't understand them, was very confused.

To make things worse, he was
chained to the temple.
As he stood there,
crowds gathered
to stare at him.

Gulliver was just as amazed.
It was like a toy town.

Chapter 2

The emperor

As soon as the emperor of the land heard about the giant man, he came to see Gulliver. But they couldn't understand each other either.

"I need to think about this," said the emperor. Leaving his soldiers to guard Gulliver, he strode off.

Everyone wanted a closer look at the giant. But some men fired more arrows at him.

"Stop that!" cried the soldiers, seizing the men.

"Here!" one shouted. "Let's give them to the giant to punish."

Gulliver picked up one of the
troublemakers and opened his
mouth. The little man wriggled
and howled with terror. He was
sure he was going to be eaten.

Meanwhile, the emperor was thinking hard. What should he do about Gulliver? He decided to ask his advisors.

"Anything that big MUST be dangerous," said one.

But, as they were talking, two men arrived. They were full of news about the men who had fired arrows at Gulliver.

The emperor was delighted. "Let's keep him," he said. "Give him plenty of food, make him some new clothes and teach him our language."

Soon, Gulliver had everything he needed. But he was still held in the temple, like a prisoner.

Chapter 3

Freedom

Gulliver learned the people's language as quickly as he could. Then he asked to see the emperor.

"Please set me free," he pleaded.

The emperor wasn't sure. "You'll have to wait," he said. "You may still be dangerous." And he sent his men to search Gulliver's pockets.

They found his handkerchief...

his snuff box...

his notebook...

his comb...

his watch...

and a bag
of coins.

The only dangerous thing
they found was his gun. But
they didn't know what it was.

The emperor wasn't satisfied. He sent a message to Gulliver.

"Do you have any weapons? Show us!" he demanded.

This is my sword!

"Don't worry," Gulliver said. "You can have them." He handed his sword and gun to the guards and the emperor relaxed. But he still didn't set Gulliver free.

Gulliver just had to wait.
To pass the time, he learned more
about the country, which was
called Lilliput. It had some very
strange customs.

One was the game of "Leaping
and Creeping". Even important
nobles played it. They had to leap
over a stick or creep under one. The
winners won prizes.

To work for the emperor, people had to do tricks. The top jobs went to the best acrobats.

Up, up and over!

Gulliver thought this custom was very odd, but he didn't show it. If he was friendly, they might trust him and let him go.

Every day, Gulliver begged to be allowed to leave the temple. Finally, the emperor agreed.

"Let him go," he declared. "The giant may walk where he likes. But he must ask first. And he must stay on the main roads!"

"I will!" Gulliver promised.

Free at last, Gulliver set off to explore the city. All the people stayed indoors, to avoid his enormous feet.

Gulliver thought he'd visit the palace, but the gate was too small and the walls were too tall. So, he cut down a tree from the palace garden and made two stools.

With a stool on either side of the wall, he could step over into the palace courtyard.

Inside, he was taken to meet
the empress and her children.

"Welcome," said the empress.
She held out her hand for
Gulliver to kiss.

Gulliver explored the entire city
before he returned to his temple
that night. When he fell asleep, he
had a smile on his face.

Chapter 4

War!

Lilliput seemed like a peaceful place but Gulliver soon found out it wasn't. One day, the emperor's secretary came to see him.

"We have a problem," he said. "There are two groups of people in Lilliput. The Tramecksans wear high heels and the Slamecksans wear low ones. They're bitter enemies and both groups want to rule."

"The emperor likes low heels at the moment, so the Slamecksans have more power. But if he changes his mind, war could break out!"

"That's terrible!" said Gulliver.

"And that's not all!" cried the secretary. "We're already at war, with a nearby island called Blefescu."

Blefescu is going to attack us!

"Why?" said Gulliver. "Whatever happened?"

"It's all about eggs," explained the secretary. "Boiled eggs and a cut finger."

Gulliver was astonished. "Eggs!" he said. "How?"

Ouch!

The secretary blushed. "Well, many years ago, everyone opened their eggs at the big end. But then the prince cut his finger when breaking his egg open."

"His father passed a law at once. No one was to crack their eggs at the big end, ever again. Eggs always had to be eaten from the smaller end."

"Lots of people refused to obey the law. They were ready to die over it and some were killed. But others fled to Blefescu, because there people still cracked their eggs at the big end."

"We've been at war ever since. And now, the Blefescu fleet is going to invade Lilliput. You have to help us," the secretary pleaded. "Please!"

All those who open their eggs at the big end: charge!

Gulliver listened carefully to the sad tale. "I'll see what I can do," he said.

He tried to find the island of Blefescu with his telescope. It was easy to spot. A fleet of ships was getting ready to set out. Gulliver counted over fifty warships.

"I'll need ropes and iron bars," he told the emperor.

Gulliver twisted the ropes together to make them stronger. Then he bent the iron bars into hooks.

"Now for the next stage of my plan," he muttered, heading to the sea. Gulliver waded in and swam almost to Blefescu.

When he rose out of the sea, towering above them, the sailors screamed with fright. Many dived overboard, just to escape.

Gulliver hooked a rope to each
of the ships and tied the ropes
together. Then he hauled the fleet
back across the sea to Lilliput.

Chapter 5

Gulliver in danger

But the emperor of Lilliput wasn't satisfied. "I want to take over Blefescu," he told Gulliver.

Gulliver thought that was going too far. "I won't make people into slaves," he said.

This made the emperor cross.
Then some messengers arrived from
Blefescu, hoping to make peace.
When they met Gulliver, they
invited him for a visit.

This made the emperor furious.
"Hrmph," he said, crossly. "I
suppose you can go. If you must."

Gulliver thought he'd better stay in Lilliput and try to keep the emperor happy.

He stayed quietly in his temple until, one night, he was woken by shouting.

"HELP! Gulliver! The palace is on fire!"

People were frantically fighting
the fire, but flames were licking the
roof. Gulliver, who was taller than
the tallest ladder, threw water over
the palace to save it.

After this, the emperor was happy again for a while. Gulliver began to enjoy life, although he kept thinking of home. But most people were very kind to him.

Three hundred tailors made him a new blue suit...

...and three hundred chefs cooked him tasty meals every day.

One evening, the emperor even visited Gulliver with his family. They all sat down to a wonderful feast at Gulliver's table.

But Gulliver's problems didn't go away. Flimnap, who was in charge of the emperor's money, didn't like Gulliver. He said he cost too much.

The emperor listened to what Flimnap said. It was true. Gulliver was very expensive.

Late one night, Gulliver had a visitor, an important noble from the palace. He kept his face hidden.

He had come with a warning. "Flimnap is turning everyone against you."

"Your enemies have written a list of your crimes. They say you're a traitor," he said.

"Even worse, they say you're plotting against the emperor. They want you killed."

"Flimnap wants to set your temple on fire and shoot poisoned arrows at you!"

Gulliver turned pale.

"Not all of the nobles want to kill you," the man added. "Some say you should only be blinded."

"But even the emperor wants to give you less food, to save money. You must leave. Now!"

Chapter 6

Escape plans

Gulliver didn't waste any time. Quickly, he scribbled a letter to the emperor.

"I'm off to visit Blefescu, as I promised," he wrote.

Then he hurried down to the sea and undressed. He piled his clothes onto the biggest ship he could find and waded into the sea between Lilliput and Blefescu.

Gulliver didn't stop until he had reached Blefescu. The king himself came out to meet him. Gulliver lay down to kiss his hand.

"Welcome!" cried the king. "Stay as long as you like."

I'm very grateful, your majesty.

Walking on the beach a week later, Gulliver spotted something strange out at sea.

It looks like a boat...

It was a small boat – but a full-sized one – floating upside down in the water.

Gulliver rushed to the king. "Please help me!" he begged.

"This could be my chance to go home. Can you help me rescue the boat?"

"Of course," said the king. "Take some ships to help you."

Gulliver swam out to the boat, holding ropes from each of the ships.

With the ships pulling and Gulliver pushing, the boat was brought safely to shore.

Gulliver set about fixing the boat for his long journey home. While he carved a tree trunk to make a mast, some of the king's men made a new sail.

The sail was like a quilt, made of thirteen layers of the strongest fabric in the land.

Soon, the boat was finished. "I'd like to leave now," Gulliver told the king. "But no one at home will believe my story. Could I take some of your people with me?"

I think your people would enjoy seeing my country.

"I can't possibly allow that," said the king. "But you may take some cows and a sheep or two."

He also gave Gulliver fifty bags of gold coins. "I don't want you to go," he said. "But I understand why you have to."

"Thank you," said Gulliver. "I'll never forget you all."

He clambered into his boat and set sail. "Goodbye, Blefescu!" he cried. "Goodbye!"

After only a few days at sea, Gulliver saw a ship. He shouted and waved wildly, hoping the sailors would see him.

He was in luck! The lookout spotted him. The ship sailed over and picked him up.

"Where have you come from?" asked the captain.

"A place called Lilliput," said Gulliver and he showed the captain his souvenirs.

The captain was astonished. For a few gold coins and a couple of cows, he agreed to take Gulliver all the way home.

Try these other books in
Series Two:

The Fairground Ghost: When Jake goes to the fair he wants a really scary ride. But first, he has to teach the fairground ghost a trick or two.

The Incredible Present: Lily gets everything she's ever wished for... but things don't turn out as she expects.

The Clumsy Crocodile: Cassy, the clumsiest crocodile in town, is about to start her new job — as a shop assistant in a china department...

Series Editor: Lesley Sims

Designed by
Katarina Dragoslavić

This edition first published in 2002 by Usborne Publishing Ltd.,
Usborne House, 83-85 Saffron Hill, London EC1N 8RT, England.
www.usborne.com
Copyright © 2002, 1982, Usborne Publishing Ltd.